The Twelve Labors of Heracles

Books by Ross Gillies:

Androcles and the Lion

Black Bears

Blackbeard the Pirate

Dark Prophecy

George and the Dragon

Greek Mythology

Jason and the Argonauts

Knights of the Round Table

Run, Wolf, Run

The Ark

The Black Witch

The Lonely Mermaid

The Odyssey

The Rat in the Hole

The Seven Voyages of Sinbad

The Tablet of Destinies

The Twelve Labors of Heracles

The Twelve Labors of Heracles

By

Ross Gillies

The goddess Hera, for Heracles,

held malice in her heart,

Heracles fortunes were therefore,

tainted from the start.

She tried to take from Heracles,

every relationship he had,

So, she contrived to wreck his life,

by driving him mad.

Heracles' family were the most

cherished gifts in his life,

But, driven mad, he slaughtered

his children and his wife.

Regaining his senses,

he wailed in horror at his deeds,

To beg the gods for forgiveness,

in Delphi he would plead.

Advised by Pythia, the Oracle,

he went to Tiryns to serve,

His cousin, Eurystheus,

ten years of labors he deserved.

"If you carry out these ten labors

in humility and charity,

The gods will reward you

by bestowing immortality.

Heracles loathed to serve a man

he knew to be inferior,

He feared opposing his father, Zeus,

despite being superior.

"Kill the Nemean Lion,

and the beast's hide you must flay,

You must return the golden fur to me,

within thirty days.

If you are successful,

I will sacrifice a ram unto Zeus,

Should you die,

as a mourning offering it will be used.

Heracles tracked the lion

and spotted it in the valley below,

Having fletched arrows for the task,

he drew back on his bow.

He was so powerful, that no beast

could his weapon endure,

He was amazed when his arrows

bounced off the lion's fur.

His weapons were useless,

some new plans must be made,

He waited until dusk and tracked

the beast, back to its cave.

There were two entrances,

so Heracles gathered some rocks,

He stacked boulders,

and one of the exits was blocked.

In the darkness he crept up,

and clubbed the lion on the head,

Strangled the lion with his strong hands,

until it was dead.

He tried to skin it with a knife,

which was not sharp enough,

Athena observed Heracles' dilemma,

the hide was too tough.

"The secret," she told him,

"lies within the lion's paws,

To carve the golden fur from the beast,

use one of its claws."

He returned to Eurystheus,

with the lion on his shoulders,

Terrified, the king,

blocked the city gates with boulders.

From entering the city,

Heracles was thereafter forbidden,

The rest of his labors

would outside the city gates be given.

A bronze jar that was large enough

for a grown man inside,

Known as a pithos, inside it,

King Eurystheus could hide.

Heracles second labor,

was the Lernaean Hydra to slay,

Hera had raised it as an assassin,

to make Heracles pay.

Upon reaching the swamp,

mired in thick noxious fumes,

He covered his mouth with a cloth,

to mask the perfume.

He fired flaming arrows into the lair,

the spring of Amymone,

From which the Hydra would spring,

to spread terror and villainy.

He confronted the Hydra with,

Athena's golden sword in his hand,

To cut the heads from the beast,

was the method he had planned.

He began slicing off the heads,

at a slow steady pace,

Two more heads sprang forth,

to take the originals place.

Realizing the Hydra had confounded

the plans he had laid,

He sought out his nephew, Iolaus,

and asked for his aid.

"As you cut off each head,

you must then cauterize the wound,

Seal its flesh with a firebrand,

that is what I assume.

Heracles took careful aim,

he didn't want to miss,

After cutting off the heads,

he sealed the stumps with a hiss.

Slicing off the final head,

fluids gushed forth in a flood,

Heracles dipped all his arrows

in the poisonous blood.

Eurystheus was furious to learn
that Heracles had survived,
For his third labor he found a task
that would ensure his demise.
He must track the Ceryneian Hind
though valleys deep and narrow,
But the beast ran so fast,
it could outrun even an arrow.

One day Heracles spotted the beasts antlers,

glinting in the sun,

He chased the Hind throughout Greece,

but was clearly outrun.

Throughout the land of the Hyperboreans,

Istria and Thrace,

Heracles over mountains,

through forests and rivers did chase.

Finally, he found the Ceryneian Hind,

as it peacefully slept,

He crept upon the creature in silence,

and captured it in a net.

With the Hind slung over his shoulder,

he set off with his prize,

The goddess Artemis approached Him,

her eyes wide in surprise.

"Why do you have my sacred animal

slung over your shoulder?"

"Forgive me, Eurystheus ordered me

to capture it," he told her.

I must perform ten labors

as a penance for my crimes,"

"If you agree to return it,

I will not punish you this time."

Eurystheus told him the Hind

was to become part of a menagerie,

Heracles plans to return the beast

would all end in tragedy.

"I will surrender the Hind,

if you come out and take it from me,"

Eurystheus reluctantly agreed,

and exited the city quite promptly.

As he approached Heracles to secure

the Ceryneian Hind's release,

Heracles dropped the beast,

and it sprang away through the trees.

As the hind returned to its mistress,

Eurystheus strode off in a huff,

"I brought you the Hind,

but you were not quick enough."

Eurystheus was humiliated

by the escape of the Hind,

"For your next labor

the Erymanthian Boar you must find.

Against this fearsome boar,

many hunters have strived,

You may not kill the beast;

you must bring it back alive."

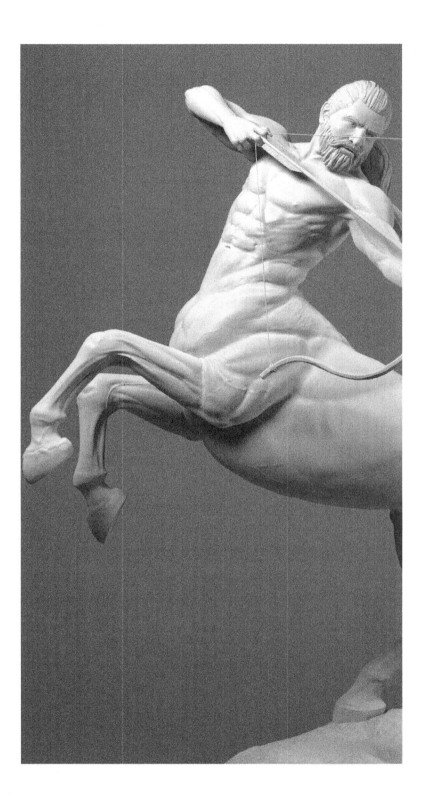

On Mount Erymanthos,

where the beast was said to dwell,

Heracles visited Pholus,

a centaur he knew very well.

After sharing a meal with his friend,

he asked for some wine,

Pholus produced a jar of wine

from Dionysus, a gift so divine.

When the jar was opened, the other centaurs,

were enticed by the smell,

But wine should be tempered with water,

a fact Heracles knew well.

Singing and dancing, the centaurs

began kicking up the leaves,

By the time the night was over,

they were all as drunk as thieves.

By the drunken centaur horde,

Heracles was brutally assailed,

Any attempt to engage in diplomacy,

very quickly failed.

With arrows poisoned by the Hydra,

many centaurs he then slew,

Submitting to the deadly missiles,

the drunken centaurs withdrew.

To discover why the arrows killed so many,

Pholus sought proof,

He picked up an arrow to examine it,

and dropped it on his hoof.

To find the cause for all this misery,

poor Pholus had tried,

He became poisoned by the arrow,

and shortly thereafter died.

Heracles visited Chiron,

how to capture the boar he would know,

"You must drive the beast into the forest,

and trap it deep in the snow."

Heracles did as he was told,

and strangled the Boar in a fight,

He returned the beast to Eurystheus,

who almost dropped dead of fright.

Eurystheus hid in his bronze pithos,

terrified of the beast,

"Take it far away from the city,

and into the wilderness release.

For your fourth labor the stables

of King Augeas you must clean,

These dung-filled stables

are the filthiest you ever have seen.

The stables have avoided

over thirty years of cleaning,"

Heracles despaired at the task;

it was really demeaning.

He demanded a reward

if he finished the task in one day,

One tenth of your thousand cattle,

to me you must pay.

Conceding that one hundred cattle,

he would gladly deliver,

Heracles washed out the stalls,

by diverting two rivers.

King Augeas refused to honor

the agreement on very specious grounds,

That Heracles by his pact,

with King Eurystheus was bound.

Augeas' son, Phylus,

supported Heracles' deposition in court,

The King banished them both,

forced them their claim to abort,

Heracles returned, slew Augeas,

and in court his case won,

As a reward he gave the kingdom,

to Augeas' son.

For the sixth labor, Heracles,

must the Stymphalian birds defeat,

Birds with beaks made of bronze,

and a rapacious appetite for meat.

The birds were sacred to Ares,

the Greek god of war,

The toxicity of their dung,

was well-known in folklore.

They migrated to Lake Stymphalia,

where they had soon quickly bred,

Destroying crops and fruit trees,

the people they struck dead.

Heracles waded into the swamp,

but very quickly became stuck,

His vast bulk was not supported,

and he was trapped in the muck.

Taking pity, Athena,

decided to assist him in his battle,

She had Hephaestus construct for him,

a magical rattle.

Heracles shook the rattle loudly,

and all the birds flew away,

Using his Hydra-poisoned arrows,

all of the birds he did slay.

He returned to Eurystheus,

and the citizens were enraptured,

For his next labor,

the Minotaur's father he must capture.

To trap the Cretan Bull,

he asked King Minos' permission,

The king's assistance was refused,

it was Heracles' decision.

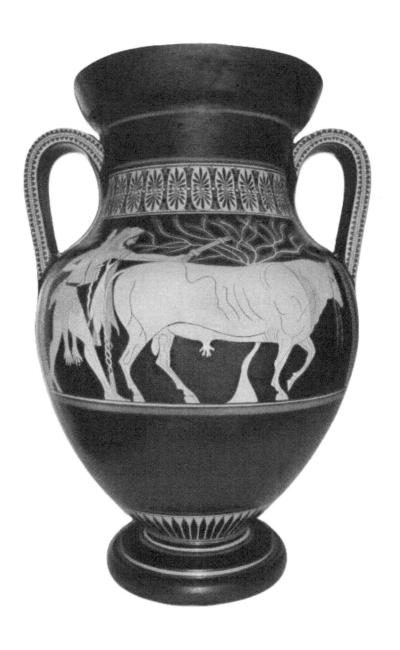

Uprooting the farmers' crops,

and destroying orchard walls,

The task of ridding them of this nuisance,

on Heracles did fall.

He tracked down the Bull,

and in silence upon it he did creep,

Throttled it with his hands,

stopping when it grew weak.

He shipped it back to Tiryns,

and Eurystheus hid out of sight,

The beast was released in Marathon,

where it grazed in delight.

The eighth of his ten labors

that Heracles was ordered to fulfil,

From Diomedes, his crazy mares,

he was commanded to steal.

The mares' madness was attributed

to their unnatural diet,

A matter about which the citizens,

were unusually quiet.

In Tirida, the mares were kept

tethered in iron chains,

Beside a bronze manger,

where the people stored grains.

They were named Lampos, Podargos,

Xanthos and Deinos,

To keep them sane the horses

were under certain embargos.

Heracles cut the beasts' chains,

after waiting for nightfall,

Diomedes launched an attack,

and Heracles fought for survival.

He slew Diomedes,

and killed the rest of his forces,

Then in a despicable act,

he fed Diomedes to his horses.

With their bellies now sated,

the mares became calm,

He tied ropes around their mouths,

so he could come to no harm.

Eurystheus demanded the mares

be sacrificed to Zeus,

But Zeus didn't want them,

and the sacrifice was refused.

The mares eventually became calm,

and roamed Argos in peace,

It was Heracles who commanded

their compassionate release.

Eurystheus' daughter, Admete,

wanted the belt of Hippolyte,

The queen of the Amazons

was considered to be very mighty.

Against the inhabitants of Paros,

Heracles' crew did defend,

Minos' sons attacked him,

and swiftly murdered his friends.

Heracles went on a rampage,

killing two of Minos' sons,

"An ignominious act

upon my companions was done."

"We will replace your crewmen,

to settle this unrest,"

Heracles inspected the men on offer,

and selected the best.

At the court of Lycus, Heracles,

his friend would protect,

He battled King Mygdon of Bebryces,

and then broke his neck.

Lycus gave thanks to his friend,

the mighty king slayer,

In honor of his brave deeds,

he named the land Heraclea.

The crew then set off for Themiscyra,

where Hippolyta lived,

Impressed by Heracles exploits,

she would to him the belt give.

Hera walked among the Amazons,

sowing seeds of mistrust,

Heracles would kidnap Hippolyta,

driven insane by lust.

The Amazons set off on horseback,

to where Heracles had gone,

Heracles assumed they had been planning

treachery all along.

"You have made a mistake," he said,

"in your attempt to betray us,"

He then slew Hippolyte,

and returned the belt to Eurystheus.

Geryon was a three-bodied giant,

on the island of Erytheia in the West,

With pasture lands and many herds

of cattle he was blessed.

For his tenth labor, Heracles,

must the giant's cattle steal,

So, he landed on the beach at Erytheia,

to settle the deal.

Orthrus was a dog,

from which two heads did grow,

It attacked Heracles, who felled it

with his club in one blow.

Eurytion, the herdsman,

came to assist his foul hound,

Heracles clubbed him on the head,

and he fell to the ground.

Geryon sprang into action,

carrying three shields and three spears,

At the river Anthemus he attacked Heracles

with loud shouts and jeers.

Heracles poisoned arrow was so forceful,

it pierced Geryon's head,

The giant bent his head over to one side,

and then fell down dead.

Herding the cattle back to Eurystheus,

he came to a river,

The river was so deep,

his cattle he could not deliver.

Heracles gathered large stones,

and into the river he did toss,

With the water now shallower,

he drove his cattle across.

At the court of Eurystheus,

his mission became clearer,

He must take the cattle to the temple,

and sacrifice them to Hera.

After Heracles completed ten labors,

Eurystheus then turned the tables,

"Killing the Hydra does not count,

nor does cleaning the stables.

Iolaus helped you in one task,

while you were paid for the cleaning,

Two more labors I will give you,"

which Heracles felt was demeaning.

"In the Garden of the Hesperides,

steal three Golden Apples from the tree."

To aid him in this quest,

Heracles captured the Old Man of the Sea.

"Oh, shape-shifting sea god,

please tell me, I pray,

Where in the world,

the Garden of the Hesperides does lay."

Arriving in the Hesperides,

he discovered a half-loaded wagon,

Filled with Golden Apples,

that were guarded by a dragon.

Affixing a poisoned arrow to his bow,

the missile he let fly,

It flew straight and true,

and struck the dragon in the eye.

Coiling and hissing,

the dragon began flailing about,

Despite its convulsions,

its demise was never in doubt.

Heracles returned to Eurystheus,

who was exceedingly glum,

Heracles had achieved something

the king thought could never be done.

The capture of Cerberus,

the three-headed dog, is your final task,

To be initiated in the mysteries

at Eleusis he would politely ask.

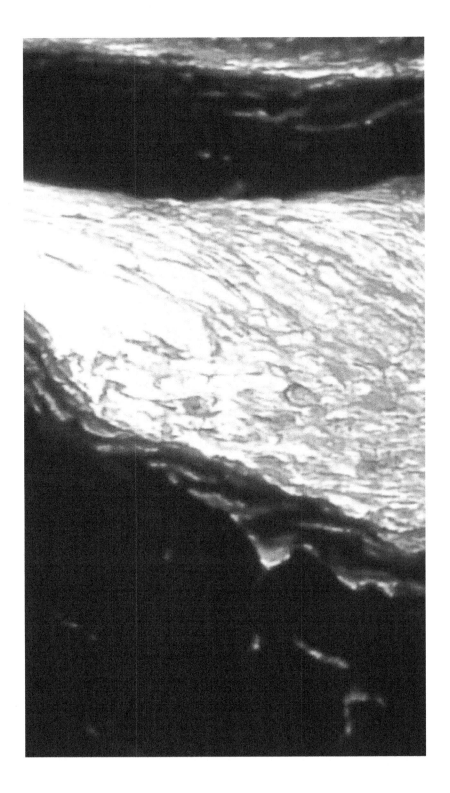

He entered the Underworld

with Athena and Hermes as his guides,

Surrounded by smoke and by fire,

he had gods at his side.

He met Theseus and Pirithous,

who by Hades had been trussed,

For trying to kidnap Persephone,

driven mad by passion and lust.

Hades had feigned hospitality,

and invited them to be seated,

They sat in chairs of forgetfulness,

and were thereby defeated.

Heracles pulled Theseus from his seat,

who was thereafter set free,

He also tried to free Pirithous,

but it was not meant to be.

Heracles asked Hades if he could take

Cerberus up to his lands,

I will allow it if you can defeat him

with your bare hands.

Heracles overpowered the dog,

and hauled it out of the cave,

Eurystheus hid in his pithos,

hoping him from the beast it would save.

"If you return the beast,

I would consider it a favor,

Complete this task and I will free you

from any further labors.

With his labors then complete,

Heracles returned to the East,

And dwelt in his homeland

in contentment and peace.

Made in United States
Orlando, FL
14 April 2022

16859227R00068